KU-175-328

Meet the
Parents

For Trudy, Alan, Freya and Tira
PB

For Jane and Dave
SO

SIMON AND SCHUSTER
First published in Great Britain in 2014 by Simon and Schuster UK Ltd
1st Floor, 222 Gray's Inn Road, London WC1X 8HB
A CBS Company

Text copyright © 2014 Peter Bently
Illustrations copyright © 2014 Sara Ogilvie

The right of Peter Bently and Sara Ogilvie to be identified as the author and illustrator
of this work has been asserted by them in accordance with the Copyright, Designs and
Patents Act, 1988
All rights reserved, including the right of reproduction in whole or in part in any form
A CIP catalogue record for this book is available from the British Library upon request

ISBN: 978-0-85707-581-9 (HB)
ISBN: 978-1-47114-512-4 (PB)
ISBN: 978-1-4711-1789-3 (eBook)
Printed in China
10 9 8 7 6 5 4 3 2 1

Meet the
Parents

Peter Bently

Sara Ogilvie

SIMON AND SCHUSTER
London   New York   Sydney   Toronto   New Delhi

Sometimes you think that your mum and your dad are there just to nag you and boss you like mad.

Do this and do that – it's a terrible bore.
But here are some MORE things your parents are for . . .

Parents are handy as mending machines
for teddies and train tracks and kneecaps and jeans.

Parents are great to build mountains of sand on,

and lovely big heaters for warming your hands on.

Parents are sofas for putting your feet up,

and dustbins for bits that you don't want to eat up.

Parents are tent poles for dens that are wonky.

Dad is a horse,

and Mum is a donkey.

Parents are targets for ketchup. And hoses.

And hunters for toys that you left in the roses.

Parents are towels for wiping your grime on.

They're whirlers and twirlers

and tree trunks to climb on.

Parents are grandstands to make you grow tall.

They're jotters

and blotters . . .

BUT that isn't all.

Parents sort out all your messes and muddles.

Parents remember.

Parents give cuddles.

Parents tell stories and tuck you up tight,
as snug as a bug in a rug every night.

Parents say 'sorry' to folks who've just met you.

They make it all better when something's upset you.

And once they have fixed all your problems . . .

and pickles,

you'd better watch out because parents love . . .

...TICKLES!